This book belongs to

_____

Bluebell Glade

Dandelion Dell

Heart of Misty Wood

Hawthorn Hedgerows

Heather Hill

Sundown Hill

Crystal Cave

Golden Meadow

Moonshine Pond

Dewdrop Spring

Honeydew Meadow

Mulberry Bushes

Misty Wood Rabbit Warren

HOME
SWEET
HOME

How many Fairy Animals books have you collected?

- Chloe the Kitten
- Bella the Bunny
- Paddy the Puppy
- Mia the Mouse
- Poppy the Pony
- Hailey the Hedgehog
- Sophie the Squirrel
- Daisy the Deer
- Kylie the Kitten
- ✓ Paige the Pony

Fairy Animals

of misty Wood

Paige the Pony

Lily Small

Henry Holt and Company
New York

With special thanks to Thea Bennett

Henry Holt and Company, *Publishers since 1866*
Henry Holt® is a registered trademark of Macmillan Publishing Group, LLC.
175 Fifth Avenue, New York, NY 10010
mackids.com

First published in the United States in 2017 by Henry Holt and Company.
Originally published in Great Britain in 2015 by Egmont UK Limited.

Library of Congress Cataloging-in-Publication Data
Names: Small, Lily, author.
Title: Paige the pony / Lily Small.
Description: First American edition. | New York : Henry Holt and Company, 2017. |
Series: Fairy animals of Misty Wood ; [book 10] | "First published in 2015 by
Hothouse Fiction Ltd." | Summary: Paige is excited about the Pony Gala and her
first chance to compete in the Prettiest Pony Competition, but is distracted by
friends who need help. Includes activities.
Identifiers: LCCN 2017028190 (print) | LCCN 2016057767 (ebook) |
ISBN 9781250127013 (Ebook) | ISBN 9781250127006 (pbk.)
Subjects: | CYAC: Fairies—Fiction. | Ponies—Fiction. | Animals—Infancy—Fiction. |
Contests—Fiction. | Conduct of life—Fiction.
Classification: LCC PZ7.S6385 (print) | LCC PZ7.S6385 Pen 2017 (ebook) |
DDC [Fic]—dc23
LC record available at https://lccn.loc.gov/2017028190

Our books may be purchased in bulk for promotional, educational, or business use.
Please contact your local bookseller or the Macmillan Corporate
and Premium Sales Department at (800) 221-7945 ext. 5442
or by e-mail at MacmillanSpecialMarkets@macmillan.com.

First American edition, 2017
Printed in the United States of America
by LSC Communications, Harrisonburg, Virginia

1 3 5 7 9 10 8 6 4 2

 Contents

CHAPTER ONE

Midsummer Morning

It was the most beautiful morning in Misty Wood, and the sun was shining high in the sky. Down in the luscious green meadow, a

little silver Petal Pony was leaping about excitedly. It was the day of the Midsummer Pony Gala, the most wonderful fairy-pony show of the year!

Paige the Petal Pony kicked her hooves high in the air and neighed happily. "I can't believe it's finally here," she said to herself, feeling the warm sunlight on her back. "The day of the Pony Gala, at last!"

2

Paige was so excited that she couldn't sit still. She'd been waiting for this special day all summer. She galloped over the grass, her pretty silvery-gray coat a blur in the sunshine.

She raced right around the meadow three times. She could have kept running all morning! But then she heard someone calling her name. "Paige!" came her mom's voice. "Where are you?"

Paige skidded to a halt. "I'm here, Mom!"

Paige's mom trotted over to the middle of the field. "You're up very early, little one," she said, nuzzling Paige hello.

"The Prettiest Pony Competition is tonight," Paige said happily. "It's always my favorite part of the gala, and I finally get to compete this year. So I've got to practice my circles!"

Then Paige leaped in the air and set off faster then ever.

Her mom laughed. "You're making my head spin! You know the Prettiest Pony Competition isn't a race, don't you?"

Paige slowed to a trot, huffing and puffing to catch her breath. Well, *that* was true. She remembered all the beautiful ponies trotting and cantering in circles last year, and leaping over

the show jumps. None of them had galloped.

Paige stood still for a moment in the warm breeze, remembering how wonderful last year's gala had been. She was sure this year's would be even better.

"Phew," Paige's mom said, a twinkle in her eye. "I couldn't think straight with you rushing around in circles like that."

Paige trotted over and

snuggled up close to her mom. "What's *your* favorite part of the gala?" she asked.

Her mom looked thoughtful. "I do love the show jumping. Your dad will be one of the judges this year. Long ago, before you were born, he was the champion show jumper!"

"Really?" said Paige, her eyes wide. "Ooh, I wonder if I could be a champion show jumper, too."

8

She bounded over to a big thistle plant and tried to jump over it. But Paige was only a little Petal Pony, and she didn't quite make it. "Ouch!" she squeaked as the prickles scratched her leg.

Her mom chuckled. "Maybe you can try the show jumps next year, when you're a bit bigger."

"Yes, I will," said Paige, instantly forgetting the scratch on her leg. "But this year, I'm going

to try for the Prettiest Petal Pony."

She pranced happily around the meadow, lifting her knees as high as she could. "Look at me! I hope the judges think I'm pretty."

Paige's mom nodded. "The judges will certainly notice a fine trot like that. But . . ."

"But what, Mom?" Paige said as she whirled around in a perfect pirouette.

". . . the judges will also be

looking for the pony with the
shiniest coat, the softest mane,
the silkiest tail, and the brightest
hooves," said her mom with a
smile. "Not to mention the kindest
heart."

Paige stopped in her tracks
and looked down at her pearly
hooves. There were grass stains on
them from all the galloping.

She shook out her snowy
mane. There were quite a few

tangles in it. She turned her head to see her coat. It was dusty with grass seeds from where she had stretched out on the ground to sleep last night.

Last of all, Paige swished her tail. It was full of pollen from all the flowers that grew nearby.

Uh-oh. Paige was a mess!

"What shall I do?" she said, worried. "I'm not very shiny or soft or silky or bright at all."

12

Paige's mom nuzzled the little pony. "You always look pretty to me, Paige. But if you want to look your best for the gala, why don't you trot over to Heather Hill? You could roll in the heather to make your coat shine."

"What a good idea!" Paige said. "And I can do my special job while I'm there."

All the fairy animals in Misty Wood had special jobs. The Petal

14

Ponies' job was to flick their tails over the flowers, wafting their beautiful scent into the air for the other fairy animals to enjoy.

"Are you coming, too?" Paige asked her mom.

"No, I'll stay here," her mom replied. "Your little sister, Pia, will be waking up any minute. But you'll be fine. Off you go and have some fun."

The two of them rubbed noses

to say good-bye, and then Paige set off for Heather Hill.

As she cantered over the meadow, a head bobbed up from the long grass. It was Petey the Pollen Puppy. "Want to have a race?" he barked.

"Sorry, Petey," Paige said, slowing down. "I've got to get ready for the Pony Gala."

"Good luck," Petey said, wagging his tail. "See you there!"

16

"See you!" Paige flicked her mane and raced on.

As she came to the edge of the wood, Daisy the Dream Deer bounded out of the trees. "Good morning, Paige!" she called in her soft voice. "Did you have sweet dreams last night?"

"Hello, Daisy," Paige called. "I did! I dreamed about the Pony Gala. I'm entering the Prettiest Pony Competition!"

Some other Dream Deer came leaping to join Daisy. "We hope you win," they cried.

"We love the gala!" And they bounded off into the wood again.

Suddenly, there was a rustle by Paige's feet, and she jumped in surprise. A pile of leaves on the ground stirred and two beady eyes peeped up at her.

It was Mia the Moss Mouse.

"Hello, Paige," Mia squeaked. "I thought I heard thunder, but it was just your hooves drumming on the ground."

"I'm hurrying to get ready for the Pony Gala," Paige explained. "I'm sorry if I frightened you."

"Ooh, I love the Pony Gala," Mia said, twitching her whiskers. "Good luck!"

Paige cantered on through

the trees until she came out on the other side of Misty Wood—and there was Heather Hill!

"Mmm," Paige sighed as she breathed in the lovely scent of the purple heather flowers.

She flicked her tail over the flowers a few times, sending the scent into the air for the other fairy animals to enjoy. Then she lay down and rolled over and over on the bouncy bushes.

21

She rubbed her coat against them, polishing it so it shone like the brightest silver. Then she stood up and gave herself a shake.

She was just about to search for a puddle to check her reflection when she heard a buzzing noise from somewhere above her head.

"Zzzzzz!"

It was *very* loud. Paige paused, her ears pricked.

"Pleazzze, pleazzze, can you help uzzz?"

Who could that be? And where was it coming from?

CHAPTER TWO

A Sticky Problem

The buzzing noise was getting even louder. "Pleazzze help uzzz, Petal Pony!"

Paige craned her silvery neck

and looked up. High in a tree, in among the branches, there was a huge swarm of bees, hovering.

Paige came to Heather Hill every day to swish her tail over the flowers, and she often met the bees flying about to gather pollen. But she'd never seen them in a huge swarm like this. They seemed to be very upset about something.

"Hello, bees," she said politely. "Is something wrong?"

25

"Yezzz!" they buzzed. "Can you help uzzz?"

"Of course," Paige said. "I'm getting ready for the Pony Gala. But I don't mind helping."

One of the bees swooped down to Paige. "Thank you so much! It'zzz our honeycomb. We've been so busy making honey for the fairy animalzzz to eat at the gala tonight—"

"Yum," Paige said. "Honey!"

"—but the honeycomb'zzz stuck inside the hive and we can't lift it out," the bee finished. "Pleazzze help!"

Paige looked up at the tree.

27

There was a beehive hanging from it. "In there?" she said, swishing at the hive with her tail.

"Yezzz," the bee said.

Paige fluttered her wings and flew onto a branch next to the hive. She poked her nose inside. Down at the bottom she could see a big honeycomb, oozing with golden honey. But she couldn't reach it.

Beating her wings gently,

Paige poked a hoof inside the hive and tried to ease the honeycomb out. But the honeycomb wouldn't budge.

"It's stuck," she told the bees.

The bees trembled with disappointment. "Oh no," they buzzed. "What a dizzzazzzter!"

"Don't worry," Paige said. "I'll just try a bit harder."

She poked her hoof in again and tried to push the honeycomb

a little more. But it still wouldn't shift. Paige fluttered her wings and pushed her hoof against it with all her might.

A moment later, the honeycomb came unstuck with a large *PLOP!*

"Huzzzah!" buzzed the bees.

Paige pushed her hoof a little more against the honeycomb, trying to ease it through the hole. With a sudden squelch, the honeycomb shot out into the air.

Paige was so surprised that she let go. She fell off the branch and tumbled onto a heather bush.

Before she had time to blink, the huge honeycomb came whizzing after her.

Slurp! It landed on her back and smashed into pieces.

"Oh no," Paige cried as the honey trickled down her sides. "It's broken!"

"Doezzzn't matter," the bees

buzzed. "There's loadzzz of lovely
honey inside the pieces. There'll
be lots and lots for the fairy
animalzzz to eat. Thank you!"

The bees flew over and lifted the pieces of honeycomb from Paige's back.

"You've been so kind," they buzzed. "Now it'zzz eazzzy for uzzz to carry. See you at the gala, Paige!"

And they flew off toward Misty Wood, each bee carrying a chunk of honeycomb.

"Good-bye, bees," Paige said, relieved she'd been able to help.

Then the little Petal Pony

looked around at her coat. A

moment ago it had been so

beautifully shiny. Now it was covered in sticky trails of honey.

She licked her shoulders, enjoying the yummy taste of the honey. She tried to lick her back and her sides, too, but she couldn't reach.

Then she tried rolling in the heather again, but instead of making her coat nice and shiny, all the twigs and leaves on the ground got stuck to the honey!

What a mess I am, Paige thought sadly, looking at her sticky, twiggy coat. *How can I clean up in time for the gala?*

She hung her head, and her snowy mane fluttered over her eyes in the sunshine.

Then Paige had a brighter thought. *If my mane looks really soft, maybe the judges won't notice my sticky coat!*

She trotted off into the forest

again, her little ears pricked. All she had to do was find somebody who could comb out her mane for her and make it look really beautiful. Then she'd be ready for the Prettiest Pony Competition!

CHAPTER THREE

Birthday Blues

Paige hadn't gone very far into
the wood when a black-and-white-
striped face popped out from
behind a tree. It was a young Bark
Badger.

Just the fairy animal I need to help me with my mane, Paige thought. She trotted over and gave a friendly flick of her head.

"Hello there," she said politely. "Could you help me get ready for the gala? I'm entering the Prettiest Pony competition and I need to look shiny and soft and silky and bright. You've got such long claws—they'd be perfect for combing my mane."

The Bark Badger shook her head. "I'm sorry," she sniffled. "I can't." She looked very unhappy.

A tear welled up and slid down her furry cheek.

"What's wrong?" Paige said softly. "My name's Paige, by the way."

"I'm Bessie," the badger said, wiping the tear away. "And I'm a very bad Bark Badger."

"You don't look bad to me," Paige said, shaking her head. "You look very kind."

The little badger sighed. "It's

my mom's birthday today, and
I haven't gotten her a present. I
want to give her one, but I can't
think what to make! She'll be so
disappointed."

"Hmm," Paige said
thoughtfully. "That is a pickle."

She remembered the lovely
present that her mom and dad
had given her for her last birthday.
They knew apples were Paige's
favorite treat, so they'd made a

great big hay-and-apple cake.

"Bessie, does your mom have a favorite thing?" Paige asked. "Something she really likes?"

Bessie wrinkled her nose, deep in thought. "Yes, she does," she said after a moment. "Mom loves leaves. Silver leaves and golden leaves, and yellowy-greeny ones, too. Oh, and red ones, of course. Especially red ones. Red is her favorite color."

44

Paige gave a little skip.
"Perfect!" she said. "I've got a
brilliant idea, Bessie. Let's make
a basket for your mom and fill it
with the brightest, prettiest leaves
we can find. What do you think?"

Bessie clapped her paws.
"That would be the best present!"

"You collect some twigs to
make the basket," Paige said.
"You'll be really good at that,
because you're a Bark Badger.

And I'll hunt for the prettiest leaves I can find."

"You're so kind," Bessie said. "Thank you!" She trundled off to find the twigs.

Paige flicked her wings and fluttered to the treetops, where masses of leaves whispered in the breeze.

This should be easy, she thought. *There must be millions of leaves up here.*

But because it was summer, most of the leaves were green. Paige had to fly a long way before she found a tree with silver leaves like shining coins.

She gathered lots of them and tucked them safely into her tail. Then she spotted a tall tree with yellowy-greeny leaves that looked like feathers. She collected lots of those, too.

Bessie's present will be amazing,

she thought. *But I must find some golden leaves, too.*

Down below, there was a

clump of bushes with tiny leaves

like drops of gold. Paige swooped

down and picked as many as she

49

could to add to her collection.

Then she remembered that Bessie's mom's favorite color was red. And Paige hadn't found any red leaves at all.

But then she spotted a beautiful crimson leaf hanging right in the middle of the bushes. "That's it!" Paige said aloud. "Perfect!"

She squeezed through the bushes, ignoring the twigs as they tugged at her mane. She pushed on

through the prickly branches until she had caught the red leaf in her teeth. Then she tried to turn back.

But she couldn't move. Her mane was tangled and twisted in the sharp twigs!

"Uh-oh," she said. "Help! I'm stuck!"

After a moment, she heard someone padding over to the bushes.

"Hello, Paige. Look what I've

made!" Bessie came hurrying up, carrying a little basket. "Oh, what are you doing in there?"

"I'm stuck," Paige said, embarrassed. She couldn't turn her head, or the twigs would pull on her mane. "I've gotten tangled up in this bush and I can't move at all!"

"Don't panic," Bessie said. "I'll have you free in a minute." She grabbed the bush and snapped

53

off the twigs until Paige was free.

"Phew!" Paige said, shaking herself out. "Thank you, Bessie. Oh—and these are for your mom." She swished her tail, and the bright leaves fell in a pile.

"They're lovely," Bessie said, jumping up and down, clapping her paws together. "You're so clever, Paige."

Bessie put the leaves in her basket. First the greeny-yellow

ones, then the ones like silver coins, then the golden ones—and finally the red leaf, right on top.

"What a beautiful basket you've made," said Paige admiringly. "And the leaves are so bright! Your mom will love her present."

"Thank you so much, Paige," Bessie said, giving her new friend a hug. "Good luck at the Pony Gala."

Bessie looked delighted as she hurried off to give the birthday gift to her mom.

Feeling happy herself, Paige called good-bye to Bessie and set off along a narrow path through the forest. It made her feel good, helping other fairy animals.

But as Paige trotted along, she felt something scratching against her neck. The broken-off twigs were still tangled up in her mane.

Oh no, she thought. *My mane looks even worse now!*

Paige was feeling very worried. How could she enter the Prettiest Pony Competition when she was such a mess? She didn't want everyone to laugh at her.

Down by the path, a little white flower was growing. It looked like a bright star against the dark soil. Paige stopped to look at it.

"Wait a minute!" she said to herself. "I'm really good at collecting things. Why don't I find lots of pretty flowers and make myself a garland? I can hang it around my neck and then no one will notice my tangled mane."

Feeling pleased, Paige twirled her wings and darted off toward Honeydew Meadow. That was where the best flowers grew!

CHAPTER FOUR

Help, We're Lost!

Paige flitted through the trees. She had to hurry. It was a long way to Honeydew Meadow, and it would take her ages to weave a garland.

Soon her shimmering fairy wings began to feel tired. *I'd better trot for a while,* she thought.

She drifted down toward a green path that wound its way through the tree trunks. As her hooves touched the ground, she heard a funny squeaking noise.

Paige pricked her ears and kept very still. The noise was coming from deep in the forest.

It sounds like someone crying, the

little pony thought. *I'd better go and see if I can help.* She stepped off the path toward the sound.

Paige had never been right in the Heart of Misty Wood before. It was shady and cool here, and the trees grew close together. The ground was muddy and her hooves sank deep into the puddles. But someone was in trouble, and she had to help them.

"Who's there?" she called softly.

"It's us," a tiny voice mewed.

"We're lost!"

Paige hurried toward the

voice. There, right in the middle

of the forest, she saw a Bud Bunny
and a Cobweb Kitten, huddled
together on top of a log.

"Bella and Chloe!" Paige said,
surprised. "What are you doing?"

"We were playing h-h-hide-

and-seek," Bella the Bud Bunny

explained in a shaky voice. "I was

looking for the best hiding place,

and I hopped all the way here.

I waited for Chloe to find me. But

it was so scary . . ."

"It took me ages to find Bella," Chloe said, her lip trembling.

"And then . . ." Bella's long ears drooped. "We realized we were lost."

"So we thought we'd wait until someone came," Chloe sniffled. "But we waited forever, and nobody did! It was horrible."

The two little friends looked so miserable. Paige had to think of something to cheer them up. She

tossed her head and gave a little prance.

"It's all right!" she said. "*I'm* here now. Jump on my back! I'll give you a ride."

"Oh, goody," Bella said gratefully, shaking her ears and bounding onto Paige's back.

"Watch out for the honey," Paige said. "I'm a bit sticky."

"Don't worry, we love honey!" Bella said. "Honey's yummy."

Chloe climbed up Paige's tail and sat beside Bella. "Watch out for the twigs in my mane!" Paige added. "Don't scratch yourselves."

"Don't worry, we'll use them to hang on to!" The kitten tucked her paws around one of the twigs.

"Ready? Off we go!" Paige called as she cantered away.

"Yay," shouted Bella, her tears forgotten. "This is great!"

"Oh yes," squeaked Chloe. "I love riding on a fairy pony!"

Paige's plan to make a flowery garland slipped right out of her mind. Instead, she pranced in little circles around the trees.

"Whoopee!" yelled Bella. "You're so bouncy, Paige."

Then Paige saw a branch
lying across the path. She
galloped up and leaped over it.
Then she jumped over it the other
way.

"Ooooh," squealed Chloe,
clinging tight to Paige's mane.
"You're a brilliant jumper!"

"How about this?" Paige said,
and twirled around in a pirouette.

"Wheeeeee!" squeaked
Bella. "You should enter the

show-jumping contest at the Pony Gala!"

"Oh yes, you'll be wonderful," Chloe agreed.

Paige stopped spinning. "Oh no!" she gasped. "I forgot about the Prettiest Pony Competition. I'm supposed to be getting all shiny and soft and silky and bright, but I'm all tangled and sticky and matted and muddy!"

"I know," Bella said.

"Why don't you drop us off at Moonshine Pond, where you can take a bath? We know the way home from there."

"That's a great idea," Paige said, relieved.

She set off through Misty Wood at her fastest gallop, with her two friends clinging tightly to the twigs in her mane.

When they got to Moonshine Pond, Bella and Chloe jumped

down from Paige's back. "See you at the gala!" Bella called.

"We hope you win the competition," Chloe added.

"Thank you!" Paige said.

As she headed over to the water, she glanced up and saw that the sun was starting to drop down below the treetops. There was no time to lose!

CHAPTER FIVE

Hunting for Hazelnuts

Before Paige could dip into
the water, she caught sight of
something red and fluffy darting
around in the bushes. It looked

like a tail. But whose tail could it be?

Forgetting the water for a moment, Paige trotted closer. The tail was wriggling about, as if it was attached to someone who was very busy indeed.

Suddenly, the tail was gone, and a face with two beady brown eyes popped up in its place.

A Stardust Squirrel!

"Hello," the squirrel said, with

76

a worried look in his eyes. "I'm Sammy."

"I'm Paige," the Petal Pony said. "Is everything all right?"

"No," the squirrel replied in a very serious voice. "Everything is not all right. In fact everything is all *wrong*!"

"Oh, dear," Paige said. "What happened?"

"I've lost something VERY important indeed. Ah—hold on!"

Sammy darted toward a clump of grass. "Maybe this is the place!"

He started digging. Soon he had dug such a deep hole that Paige could only see his back legs and tail. Then Sammy wriggled out again with a blob of dirt on the end of his nose.

"Nothing!" he said. "This is terrible. Worse than terrible." He looked at Paige and twitched his nose. "What's worse than terrible?"

HUNTING FOR HAZELNUTS

"Er, horrible?" Paige suggested.

"Yes, it's terrible and horrible—terri-horrible," Sammy said. "I wonder—would you be very kind and help me? If you help me, we might find them and then this *wouldn't* be the worst day of my life ever."

"Of course!" Paige said. "But what are you looking for?"

Sammy had started digging again. Earth and stones flew up like a fountain behind his busy paws.

"My *hazelnuts*, of course!" he said. "I buried them last autumn. Right here, on the bank of Moonshine Pond. And now I can't find a single one."

He scratched his head, looking very puzzled. "I've *got* to find them. My friends and I are going to the Pony Gala this evening and we're supposed to be having a picnic. But we won't have anything to eat if I can't find my hazelnuts."

81

"I'm going to the Pony Gala, too," Paige said, suddenly remembering what she was *supposed* to be doing. "I'm in the Prettiest Pony Competition."

"Oh." Sammy sat back on his hind legs and looked her up and down.

"I know I look really messy," Paige told him, feeling embarrassed. "But every time I try to make myself look prettier,

82

something happens to make me even messier!"

"Well—your tail looks very pretty!" Sammy said. "It's so long and silky and white."

"Thank you!" Paige said and felt better. Poor Sammy—he was so worried about his picnic. Surely it wouldn't take long to find a few hazelnuts?

"How can I help?" she asked.

"Well," Sammy said, "those

83

hooves of yours would be great for digging."

Paige nodded. "They are. Do you have any idea where your hazelnuts might be buried?"

"No," Sammy said sadly. "It was somewhere on the bank, but I just don't know *where*."

Paige thought for a moment. "My mom loses things sometimes. Like our apples. She hides them under the hedge or behind a tree

trunk to keep them safe, and then she can't find them. 'I put those apples in a very safe place,' she says, 'And now I can't remember where that safe place is!'"

Sammy nodded. "That's just like me. My hazelnuts are very precious indeed. I always look for a safe place to hide them."

"Well, maybe what we need to do is to look all around Moonshine Pond for the safest place," Paige

suggested. "I bet your hazelnuts

will be there."

"Good idea!" exclaimed

Sammy. "What about under

those tree roots?"

Paige followed

him to a big

tree near the

pond. She

scraped the

earth away

with her hooves,

but there were no hazelnuts hidden under the roots.

"What about those reeds by the water?" Paige said. "Maybe you hid the hazelnuts between the stems."

"Good thinking!" Sammy cried, and the two of them rummaged around among the reeds, but still they couldn't find the hazelnuts.

"This is hopeless," Sammy

87

groaned. "We'll never
be able to have
our picnic."

"Wait a minute."
Paige looked across
Moonshine Pond.
"You see that place where the bank
hangs over the water? That's the
safest place ever. I bet you hid
them there!"

She cantered over to the very
edge of the pond.

"Careful!" Sammy called, scampering along. "Don't fall in!"

It was hard, leaning over and digging at the bank with her hooves. But Paige knew it was the best place to find the hazelnuts.

And sure enough, there they were—lots of tasty brown nuts, gently wrapped in leaves to keep them clean, tucked away inside the bank.

"Sammy, I found them!"

Paige called. But she was so excited that she slipped on the muddy bank and lost her balance. "Help!" she squealed as she slid toward the squelchy brown mud.

Sammy fluttered up and grabbed her mane in his teeth. "Steady!" he said. "I've got you."

Paige clambered back onto the grass.

"Thank you, you're so kind!" Sammy chattered as he gathered up the hazelnuts one by one. "This is going to be the best picnic ever! See you at the gala, Paige! Good luck!"

And he rolled up the nuts in a

lily pad and rushed off to find his friends.

Paige went to wave good-bye to him with her tail, but it felt really heavy. "Oh no," she cried as she looked over her shoulder. Her tail was soaking wet and covered in chocolatey-brown mud.

"Drrrrrr! Drrrrrrr!" A loud noise boomed through the wood.

Paige pricked her ears. The woodpeckers were drumming a

message on the tree trunks. The Pony Gala was about to begin!

She looked down at her reflection on the smooth surface of the pond.

I look messier that ever! she thought. Her coat was sticky. Her mane had twigs in it. Her hooves were muddy—and now her tail was, too!

High in the sky there was a tweeting sound. Paige looked up

93

to see a beautiful bluebird flying

overhead.

"It's gala time!" the bluebird

tweeted. "Make your way to

Golden Meadow!"

I can't, Paige thought sadly.

I'm just too messy and scruffy. She would simply have to miss out on the Prettiest Pony Competition this year.

At least, she'd have to miss out on *entering* the competition.

I can still watch, I suppose, Paige mused. *I just need to find a good spot where nobody will see me.*

CHAPTER SIX

A Very Special Prize

Paige peeped out from behind a

mossy tree trunk at the edge of

Golden Meadow. It was the perfect

97

hiding spot for a little Petal Pony,
right behind the judges' panel for
the Prettiest Pony Competition. She
could see everything, but she was

pretty sure no one could see her.

The show jumping had just finished. The winner was Pippin, a pony with a coat like a shiny brown chestnut. Paige's dad was presenting the prize to him—a huge cake made of apples and heather.

"Yippeee!" cheered all the ponies that were watching. "Great win, Pippin!"

"Yay, well done!" shouted all the fairy animals in the crowd.

99

Paige wished she could join in with the shouting and cheering. But she was too shy to go anywhere near the Pony Gala when she looked such a mess.

Then she heard a familiar little whinny. Her baby sister, Pia, was trotting across the meadow, right near Paige's hiding spot.

Pia looked so cute, with her mane and tail as fluffy as a dandelion clock. Paige wanted to

100

go and rub noses with her, but she couldn't leave the tree trunk.

"Daddy! Have you seen Paige?" Pia asked.

"No, I haven't," their dad replied. "It's nearly time for the Prettiest Pony Competition, and we don't want her to miss out! Let's see if we can find her."

Paige's heart skipped a beat. But then the two of them trotted away toward the crowd. Her hiding place was safe.

In the middle of the meadow, a team of Cobweb Kittens was stretching a rope of cobwebs

into a big circle for the Prettiest Pony Competition. They hung shimmering dewdrops all along it.

Beautiful Petal Ponies began trotting into the ring, their silky manes and tails floating in the air. Their eyes shone with excitement as the crowd started cheering. Paige caught sight of her friend Poppy, her blue wings sparkling in the sunlight.

Little Pia cantered up to the

judges' panel. "You have to stop the competition," she squeaked at the judges. "Paige is missing and we can't find her anywhere."

"Oh, dear," said one of the judges, a regal brown pony with white patches. "We can't keep everyone waiting. Do you know where she is?"

Paige's mom hurried across the ring. "Perhaps she's just forgotten . . ."

Pia shook her head. "Paige wouldn't forget. She's been looking forward to it all summer."

Paige's friend Poppy trotted over, looking confused. "Where is Paige? She said she'd be here."

Then Pia began to cry. "Where is she?"

Paige couldn't bear to see her baby sister so upset. She took a deep breath and leaped out from her hiding spot.

"I'm here," she said softly,
cantering over to the judges.

"Hooray!" Pia said, rushing
over to rub noses with Paige as
Poppy sighed with relief.

Pia didn't seem to notice her sticky coat and tangled mane and muddy hooves and slimy tail. "I'm so glad you're all right," Pia whispered.

The other judge, a coal-black pony, tossed her mane importantly. "Now that all our contestants are here," she said, "we may begin the Prettiest Pony Competition!"

As the two judges called all the ponies into the ring, Paige turned

107

to her mom and Pia. "I'm still not ready," she told them fretfully.

"You always look beautiful to me," her mom said, nuzzling her. "Now go out there and show them how pretty you are, on the inside and out!"

Paige took a deep breath and trotted into the ring with Poppy and the other ponies. She arched her neck, skipped around, and kicked her hooves in the air. Pretty

A VERY SPECIAL PRIZE

soon, she was having so much fun that she'd forgotten about how messy she looked.

In the crowd, she could see Petey the Puppy and Daisy the Deer and Mia the Mouse. They were all waving and smiling at her. Everyone was watching, but Paige didn't mind.

This is so much fun, she thought as she did a perfect pirouette. *Who cares if I'm scruffy and messy?*

110

I'm just glad to be here with Poppy and Pia and all these beautiful Petal Ponies.

When the judges were ready to announce their winner, the ponies stopped prancing and the crowd burst into applause. The Petal Ponies stood still, beaming, as the black pony judge stepped forward. The crowd fell silent.

"This has been a particularly exciting year for the Prettiest Pony

Competition," the judge said.
"And we'd like to congratulate the
winner, a beautiful young pony by
the name of . . ."

Paige held her breath. She
couldn't win—could she?

". . . Poppy!" the judge
finished, and the crowd went wild.

Paige cheered just as loudly
as everyone else, delighted for her
friend. She hardly minded that she
hadn't won, because Poppy was

112

indeed a very beautiful pony, and a very good friend as well.

The judges pinned a red rosette to Poppy's mane and presented her with her prize—a huge cake made of carrots and honey. Poppy's golden coat shone, and her hooves were as bright as pearly shells. She deserved to win the prize.

Everyone cheered and clapped as Poppy trotted around

prettily with her honey-and-carrot cake. Paige and the other ponies cantered out of the ring to watch.

As Paige stood there on the sidelines, she heard a loud buzzing noise. A swarm of bees was flying across the ring—coming straight toward her! They were carrying a piece of honeycomb, shaped just like a flower, which they laid carefully on Paige's head. It smelled lovely.

"This izzz to say thank you for being so kind," they buzzed.

Then Bessie the Badger came lolloping over the grass, carrying a comb made from birch bark. "You were so wonderful, Paige," she said. "Thank you for helping me with Mom's present—she really likes it. I've made you a comb for your mane!"

"It was no trouble," Paige told them. "I enjoyed helping."

She lowered her head so that Bessie could comb away the twigs and tangles. Then Bessie fixed the comb in Paige's mane, just behind the honeycomb flower.

Then Chloe and Bella hurried over. Chloe had a big basket with her, and Bella was carrying a garland of pink and blue flowers.

"I hope we're not too late," Chloe mewed as she sprinkled dewdrops from the basket over

Paige's coat and rubbed until all the sticky honey was gone. Then she washed Paige's muddy hooves so they were shiny again.

"Oh, that's lovely," Paige said softly. She didn't tell Chloe the competition was over, and that Poppy had won. She didn't want to hurt her feelings.

Bella fluttered in the air and placed the flower garland around Paige's neck. "Thanks for helping

118

us," she said. "We'd never have gotten home safely without you."

"You're welcome," Paige said with a smile.

Then someone scampered up behind her. "Hi there," Sammy chirped as he scattered sparkling stardust all over Paige's tail. "I just had to come and say thank you for helping me find my hazelnuts—our picnic was delicious!"

A big cheer went up from all

119

the Stardust Squirrels in the crowd.
Paige looked up, and realized that
the other fairy animals had gone
silent.

Everyone was looking over at
her curiously, including Poppy,
who'd finished her winner's circuit.

"There," Sammy said when
he'd finished. "You really are the
prettiest pony now."

Paige blushed, suddenly
feeling shy. The two judges came

over to see what was happening.

"What beautiful decorations!" the regal brown pony said, looking closely at the honey flower and the bark comb.

"Indeed!" The black pony nodded, admiring the garland and the shimmering stardust. "It's a shame the competition is over. You look very pretty, Paige!"

"Oh no," mewed Chloe. "We *were* too late!"

121

"I'm sorry," said Bella, her ears drooping.

"Me, too," said Bessie.

"Oh no," Sammy sighed.

"Dizzzaster," buzzed the bees. "We should have come faster!"

But the black pony shook her head. "We couldn't help overhearing what your friends were saying," she said. "And being kind is just as important as being pretty. So we've decided to

122

award you a very special prize.
Congratulations, Paige, for being
the Kindest Pony in Misty Wood!"
Then she pinned a beautiful red
rosette onto Paige's mane and
gave her a basket filled with red
apples.

"Ooh," Paige said. She was
so happy she could hardly speak!
She squeaked out, "Thank you!"
The crowd around them started
cheering.

123

"Hooray, Paige! Well done, Paige!" roared the crowd as she beamed and tossed her silky mane.

Later that afternoon, after the gala was over, Paige and her family stood under a shady tree and shared the apples as the sun went down.

"I'm so proud of you," Pia said, cuddling up to Paige.

Paige's dad swished his tail

happily. "So am I!" he said. "You
entered the competition even
though you hadn't had time to get
ready. You knew you wouldn't win,
but you still took part."

"You're the Kindest Pony," Paige's mom said, "and that makes me the proudest mom! Well done, Paige."

Paige felt all warm and happy inside. She thought of the friends she had helped today, and how they had helped her, too.

"I just did what any good fairy animal would do," she said happily, and crunched into one of the delicious red apples.

128

Turn the page for
lots of fun
Misty Wood
activities!

Spot the Difference

The picture on the opposite page is slightly different from this one. Can you circle all the differences?

Hint: There are six differences in this picture!

Maze

Help Paige get to the Prettiest Pony competition and win the prize apples!

Fairy Animals
of Misty Wood

Meet more Fairy Animal friends!

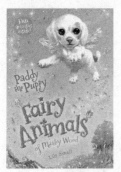

Paddy the Puppy
Fairy Animals
of Misty Wood
Lily Small

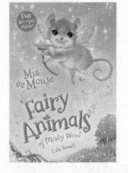

Mia the Mouse
Fairy Animals
of Misty Wood
Lily Small

Poppy the Pony
Fairy Animals
of Misty Wood
Lily Small

Hailey the Hedgehog
Fairy Animals
of Misty Wood
Lily Small

Sophie the Squirrel
Fairy Animals
of Misty Wood
Lily Small

Daisy the Deer
Fairy Animals
of Misty Wood
Lily Small

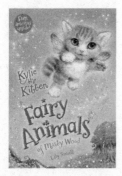

Kylie the Kitten
Fairy Animals
of Misty Wood
Lily Small

Paige the Pony
Fairy Animals
of Misty Wood
Lily Small